BIONICLE®

WORLD

by Greg Farshtey

BIONICLE®

FIND THE POWER,
LIVE THE LEGEND

The legend comes alive in these exciting BIONICLE® books:

BIONICLE®

WORLD

by Greg Farshtey

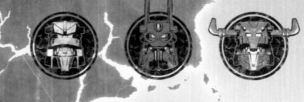

SCHOLASTIC INC.

NEW YORK   TORONTO   LONDON   AUCKLAND   SYDNEY

MEXICO CITY   NEW DELHI   HONG KONG   BUENOS AIRES

ISBN-13: 978-0-439-78796-3
ISBN-10: 0-439-78796-3

12 11 10 9 8 7 6 5 4 3 2   8 9 10 11/0

Designed by Cheung Tai
Printed in the U.S.A.
First printing, April 2007

Contents

INTRODUCTION

It is with a heavy heart that I sit down to carve these words into stone. As a founding member of the Order of Mata Nui — a secret organization dedicated to serving the will of the Great Spirit Mata Nui — I have seen the ongoing war between light and darkness in our universe. But never have we seemed so close to the end of all things.

And so I am creating this chronicle with the very latest information on eleven key locations. These are the places that have been critical to recent events, or may be drawn into the battles to come. Some are sites to turn to in times of crisis, others spots to avoid, for they are nests of evil.

When it is done, these tablets will be shared with the rest of the Order and our agents. Information we feel is vital for the Toa to have will be revealed to them in such a way that they cannot know the source. And should we fail — and the universe fall — then this may well be the final record of these lands and their people.

A NOTE ON OUR AGENTS

Vital information for the entries in this book was provided by three of our agents – Jerbraz, Tobduk, and Johmak – based on their personal memories of the sites involved or the legends they have heard. Thus the style of the carvings we have included may vary, as each worked in his own way and based his creation on varying levels of information. The Order can rest assured that each carving is as accurate as it was possible to be.

CHAPTER ONE

ARTAKHA

It may seem strange to begin this atlas with the location about which we know least — but as Artakha was the very first island created in our universe by the Great Beings, it seems the only place to begin.

For most Matoran, Artakha is a name that lives only in legend. According to the tales, at a time when the universe was new, Matoran labored in darkness. They had no true idea what they were working on or why. Those Matoran who showed particular promise were allowed to travel to Artakha and work in the light. Since then, the island has been thought of as a refuge, a place where Matoran would be safe from harm.

But Artakha is far more than just a safe haven.

GETTING THERE

The easy answer to this is, no one knows. At one time, ages ago, there was a land bridge that connected Artakha to a larger uninhabited island, and the locations of both were marked on various maps and charts. Then the Brotherhood of Makuta struck. They invaded the island and stole a valuable artifact. After that, at the request of Artakha's ruler, the Order of Mata Nui stepped in and destroyed every known existing chart or map that showed its location (including any of our own). The land bridge and the other island were eliminated by Artakha's inhabitants. And all of those who knew where Artakha was — among them members of the Order and various servants of the Brotherhood — were made to disappear.

It is possible that somewhere within our Order or within the Brotherhood, there exists a being or beings who know Artakha's location. If so, they are too smart to admit it out loud.

Not so very long ago, two Matoran on the island of Mata Nui started a quest to find Artakha. They failed and turned back. This was fortunate . . . for them.

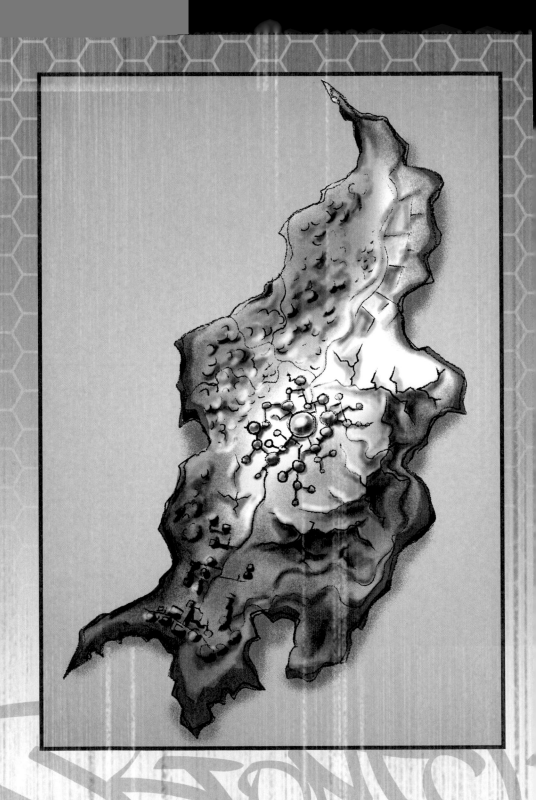

THE LAND

No single description can capture Artakha. Even the illustrations we have placed in this volume encompass only one aspect of the land. Artakha is different on every visit, or at least always used to be when outsiders were allowed there. The topography and plant life, and even some aspects of the climate, change seemingly at random. Artakha can go from beautiful and idyllic one moment to dark and forbidding the next, depending on what impression its ruler seeks to make.

HISTORY

Artakha was one of the first two islands to come into being in this universe (the other being Karzahni). It was created from nothing by the Great Beings and was tasked with overseeing the birth of much of the rest of what we now know as our world.

Once the universe was whole, the island's inhabitants turned their attention to creating artifacts that would be vital in millennia to come. Here the Great Kanoka Disks were forged, as well as the Kanohi Mask of Shadows now worn by the Makuta of Metru Nui. It was also here that the first Toa came into being. Her name is lost to history, but it is known that she was a Toa of Water and had some involvement with the building of the city of Metru Nui.

Easily one of the most important objects created on Artakha was the Kanohi Avohkii, the Great Mask of Light. Although no Toa of Light existed to wear it at the time, the mask was considered to be insurance against the day the Brotherhood of Makuta might choose to rebel. If that day came, only the power of light would be able to stand against the shadow.

Of course, as we now know, that rebellion did take place. But the Brotherhood knew of the existence of the Avohkii, and so they struck at the island of Artakha. Their strike team of Rahkshi and Visorak, led by a Brotherhood member, easily overcame all defenses and took the Mask of Light.

Some of the consequences of this disaster have already been noted above. Artakha became isolated, with its creations — such as the Kanohi Nuva masks — delivered anonymously and in mysterious ways. How the island's inhabitants know what is needed, and where, is unknown even to us.

Here the history of Artakha must stop. No outsider has been allowed on the island for ages, so we can only assume that all is as it once was there. It is disturbing to realize that if some natural cataclysm were to destroy Artakha, none of us would ever know.

THE INHABITANTS

ARTAKHA

The ruler of the island, Artakha is a figure of legend. It is said that he has never been seen in all the time that he has reigned there. There have been stories, of course — that he was a Great Being, that he was the Great Spirit Mata Nui himself, and on and on, typical Matoran mythology. As far as we can tell, none of those tales is true. But exactly what Artakha is, we cannot say.

One thing that is certain is that he has great talent as a designer and builder. The present-day look of cities like Metru Nui is largely credited to his influence. Many of the weapons used by the earliest Toa were also crafted by him or the Matoran who work for him. Ancient legend states that those who wished the impossible built could leave raw materials at the gate of his fortress, and return in the morning to find the item they desired.

One persistent myth is that Artakha wears a mask designed by the Great Beings, a Kanohi Mask of Creation. While it does not actually bring things into being, it helps the wearer to envision how they should look and how they should be designed. According to the legend, only one such mask exists, and Artakha and Karzahni competed for the right to wear it. Karzahni lost, perhaps in part explaining why his efforts to heal damaged Matoran met with such disastrous failure (see Chapter Two).

THE MATORAN

The Matoran who populate Artakha were, at one time, perhaps the most content in all the universe. They were laboring in peace, with all the materials and tools they could ever want. They were doing interesting work that contributed to the greater good. Although living well away from other populated lands, they had visitors from other places to keep them informed about the world beyond.

We can only guess how much that has changed since Artakha's borders were closed. The Matoran are still working, but how much they know or understand about what they are building and why is unknown. It is possible that only Artakha truly knows the reasons for their labors and only he ensures that artifacts get to where they are needed. His millennia of seclusion would seem to indicate he is not known for sharing anything — especially awareness, even of himself — with others. Perhaps he sees it as enough that they are busy, at peace, and willing to follow his direction in all things.

CREATURES OF ARTAKHA

CRYSTAL SERPENTS

At the dawn of time, Artakha is said to have decided that he could create Rahi as easily as masks or weapons. His first and only attempt resulted in the creation of four great crystal serpents. Unlike ordinary reptiles that relied on biting or crushing their prey, the crystal serpents required only light to attack or defend. Maneuvering so that direct light hit them, they could amplify that light through their crystalline forms until it became a lethal heat ray.

Realizing that these creatures could not be tamed, yet unwilling to destroy his own creations, Artakha set them free and gave up on trying to create living things. The four serpents migrated to four different parts of the island, and today occupy the northern, eastern, southern, and western sections. They are dormant most of the time, sleeping underground or in the shade of great boulders. It is believed they need to feed only once every two centuries or so. Although

Matoran is not their preferred dish, the villagers always considered it wise to be elsewhere when the serpents were awake and active.

UPDATE

With so little information on the current state of Artakha, it is difficult to provide an update. However, recent events — particularly on Voya Nui — may soon force us to seek out the island of Artakha. It is rapidly becoming impossible to stake the future of the universe on a ruler and people with whom we have no contact and about whom we know next to nothing. We may well come to need Artakha's resources at our disposal, rather than simply whenever that island's inhabitants choose to share them.

KARZAHNI

Every light must have a corresponding shadow. Artakha is a place of refuge for the Matoran, while the realm of Karzahni has become a place of exile and doom.

Situated in a rarely traveled area south of the island city of Metru Nui, Karzahni was created along with Artakha in the first days of the universe. At the time, it could be reached by sea as well as by land, but the water routes have long since dried up. The region is now landlocked and the sole surviving access route is treacherous in the extreme.

It is not a place one visits by choice . . . and it is not a place one ever leaves.

GETTING THERE

The overland route to Karzahni travels through a barren wasteland that has claimed the life of more than one Toa over the centuries. A tunnel that devours light leads to an archway through which no one with the power of light can pass. The mountain road that leads from there to Karzahni itself is guarded by monstrous crab creatures called Manas, and haunted by the tragic Matoran inhabitants of this land.

THE LAND

Karzahni's geography is as twisted as the heart of its ruler. Fire provides no warmth, while the touch of ice burns. Dust falls cascade over mountains while pools of water sit unmoving. Thunder makes no noise, but the sound of a gentle breeze can be deafening.

Karzahni rests in the middle of a bowl-shaped canyon. The pathways leading to it are flanked by what appear to be statues of Matoran. In fact, these are Matoran turned to stone for the crime of laziness. Just as they have become rock, the rock of the pathway has become a form of life. The stones scream beneath your feet when you walk upon them.

Sitting in the middle of the realm is the fortress of Karzahni himself, the realm's ruler. While it was once a stunning landmark, it has degenerated over time into a charred ruin. The fires inside are visible from some distance away, but there is nothing welcoming about the sight.

The only other major structures are the huge forges and furnaces used to make tools and weapons and "repair" Matoran mechanical parts. Absent from the region are shelters for the Matoran who live there. They remain outdoors, exposed to the elements, with no place to rest except on hard, barren rock.

HISTORY

The realm of Karzahni came into being for a very simple reason. Matoran workers have always been among the most important inhabitants of the universe. Without them, the will of the Great Spirit Mata Nui could not be carried out. So if a Matoran is injured or for some reason is a poor worker, it is important that any damage be healed as quickly as possible. The Matoran can then be returned to the labor force ready to do his or her part. This realm was intended to be the place where injuries could be repaired and poor attitudes could be changed.

The being called Karzahni was placed in charge. His job was to welcome new Matoran who had been sent here by their village elders and to do what he could to make them good and healthy workers again. Unfortunately, it rapidly became obvious he did not know how to do that. The first Matoran sent to him did not become stronger as a result of his work — they became smaller, weaker, and strangely twisted by what he did. To compensate, Karzahni gave them weapons to defend themselves and then shipped them as far from his realm as he could so they would not be around to remind him of his failure. (These Matoran would eventually wind up on the island of Voya Nui. See Chapter Four.)

More Matoran arrived from other lands, and more failures resulted. Karzahni eventually decided the problem was not his skill — it was the Matoran themselves. It was obviously not their destiny to be repaired, but instead to be punished. Karzahni stopped even trying to make Matoran better and started imprisoning them within his realm.

After a long period of sending Matoran to Karzahni, only to never have them return, village elders stopped transporting their people to the realm. Legends grew about Karzahni as a place to which bad workers were sent, never to return, and Matoran would use the tales to frighten one another. "Go to Karzahni!" became a common phrase in their arguments.

From that time to this, only six Matoran have entered the realm. This was Jaller and his team, who were traveling from Metru Nui to Voya Nui on a quest. Thanks to the discovery of long-unused Toa transport canisters, they were able to escape the realm. But the other Matoran inhabitants are still there, doomed to remain until Karzahni is overthrown or the universe ends.

THE INHABITANTS

KARZAHNI

Powerful, almost regal, and quite insane — all three terms can be used to describe Karzahni. He has ruled the realm named after him for more than 100,000 years, and time has not made him any kinder or more merciful.

Karzahni is a huge figure, his armor battered and twisted and his mask looking like four welded together. His black and gold armor is studded with razor-sharp blades, and his gauntlets crackle with energy. His eyes are deep and black, and they gleam with madness. In one hand he carries a length of burning chain, his preferred weapon.

Although very strong, he almost never needs to strike anyone to defeat them. Karzahni has the power to make others see visions of the future. These "what ifs" usually focus on the terrible consequences if an escape attempt is tried and failed, or on some other event that will crush the target's hopes and dreams. In this way, Karzahni creates doubt and hesitation in any who oppose him. Karzahni used this power very effectively on Jaller, making him see what life would have been like had he failed to save his friend Takua from a Rahkshi attack. That vision reminded Jaller of just what could happen if he tried to fight Karzahni and lost. Now worried about the fate of his friends if he failed, he chose to surrender instead.

Note: An interesting fact about Karzahni is how little he knows about the universe around him. Because he has been in his realm since virtually the birth of the universe, he has very little knowledge about Mata Nui, the Brotherhood of Makuta, Toa, or anything else outside of his empire. It was only after Jaller and

his team arrived that he learned any of these beings existed. How he chooses to use that knowledge remains to be seen.

THE MATORAN

The Matoran prisoners of Karzahni have been in the realm for tens of thousands of years. Most, long ago, gave up any hope of escape. A small number have become willing servants of Karzahni, while the rest simply wander among the rocks, all the life gone from their eyes. All are physically damaged in some way, and most do not speak — what is there to talk about?

Although there may be a few Matoran who still have some fire inside, a visitor to Karzahni should not count on finding allies here. The Matoran are so afraid of their ruler that they will be more likely to fight you than to risk his anger.

CREATURES OF KARZAHNI

Very, very little can thrive in the barren wasteland of Karzahni. Those that do live there tend to be either large and dangerous or too small to be noticed by predators.

MANAS CRABS

Manas are huge, vicious creatures that reside in Karzahni in large numbers and serve as guards for the ruler. Why creatures that would seem to be most at home in water would choose a rocky, mountainous, and largely arid area as their home is unknown. It could be that they are evil by nature and simply feel more welcome among those who share that evil.

Unlike Manas in the wild, which tend to turn on each other at any opportunity, the Manas of Karzahni are well disciplined. The Matoran live in fear of them, and the knowledge that they guard the only way in or out of the realm is enough to discourage escape attempts.

The presence of so many Manas here means it would take an army of Toa to seize the realm, and even then, many of the Toa would not live to fight another day.

DUST DARTERS

Barely big enough to be seen by the naked eye, dust darters live in and around the dust falls. When spotted in a swarm, they look like nothing so much as a cloud of dust, which helps camouflage them from predators. Although they seem harmless, dust darters can be dangerous to longtime inhabitants of Karzahni, for they feed off of metallic protodermis. Over a long period, their feasting can weaken the armor of even a Manas or make the damage to a Matoran's mechanical parts worse. Wander far enough into Karzahni and you will hear the almost rhythmic clanging of metal against rock, the sound of dust darters being swatted by Matoran.

UPDATE

Since the escape of Jaller, Hahli, and their group from Karzahni, a change seems to have come over the ruler of this realm. Rather than ignoring the many Matoran who wander his land, he has begun actively gathering them together and training them. It almost seems as if he is trying to create an army, though for what purpose is unknown. While the Matoran of Karzahni are really no threat to anyone, if they were backed by Manas, this could be a formidable fighting force. This situation will need to be closely monitored in the future. We cannot afford distractions when the Great Spirit Mata Nui is so close to death.

CHAPTER THREE

METRU NUI

One of the most important cities in the known universe, Metru Nui has long been a prize coveted by the Brotherhood of Makuta and the Dark Hunters. Possession of the city — more importantly, control of its Matoran — would have conferred tremendous power and influence on its owner.

After being abandoned for centuries, the city is once again teeming with life. However, it remains a target for those who wish it — and the Great Spirit Mata Nui — harm.

GETTING THERE

Metru Nui is an island city, accessible by ship, airship, and through a series of ancient and unsafe underwater transport chutes. For most of the last 1,000 years, all but one of the sea gates leading to the waters around Metru Nui were closed.

The other means of access to Metru Nui is a series of tunnels that lead aboveground to the island of Mata Nui. Although these have been partially explored, they remain largely unknown and dangerous.

THE LAND

The island of Metru Nui is broken up into six districts, or metru.

Ta-Metru: Home of the mask, this district was once filled with working forges and vats of molten protodermis. Much of the metru was melted due to spillage from the vats, and only small portions are habitable.

Le-Metru: Once the transport hub of Metru Nui, this district was badly damaged by the earthquake 1,000 years ago. However, the Le-Matoran are extremely industrious and a good deal of rebuilding has already been done.

Ga-Metru: Home to scholars and teachers, Ga-Metru was best known as the site of the Great Temple. The temple was badly damaged by Toa Hordika Vakama during the Visorak invasion. It is now in the process of being rebuilt.

Onu-Metru: Site of the Great Archives, a museum/zoo featuring every creature and artifact in the city. It was shattered by the quake, allowing all the Rahi imprisoned within to escape. Onu-Matoran are hard at work rebuilding it, though it will take a great deal of time to complete the work.

Po-Metru: Least damaged of all the metru, Po-Metru consists of mountains and great barren plains. Many of the newly returned Matoran are living here while their own metru are being repaired.

Ko-Metru: At one time, this was the center of knowledge and thought in the city. But the quake toppled the crystalline Knowledge Towers, shattering them. Work is being done in the metru, but Le-Metru is currently being given priority because of the need to get the transport system up and running again.

HISTORY

As the history of Metru Nui has been well chronicled, we thought it best to use this space to provide a historical time line of events in the city. For reasons that should be well known to members of the Order, it is not complete.

100,000 Years Ago Metru Nui founded by the Great Beings, who lay its foundations. Actual construction work done by the Matoran.

87,000 Years Ago Metru Nui forges trade pact with League of Six Kingdoms.

80,000 Years Ago League of Six Kingdoms rebels and is crushed by Brotherhood of Makuta. All pacts nullified. Trade with many areas interrupted.

79,500 Years Ago The Great Disruption. Matoran civil war breaks out in Metru Nui.

79,100 Years Ago	Brotherhood of Makuta steps in to end conflict. War leaders banished to the Pit. Order of Mata Nui places agent in city to head off future problems, if possible.
79,000 Years Ago	Golden Age of peace and prosperity begins for Metru Nui.
60,000 Years Ago	Time Slip. Six-month period that no one in the universe can recall and of which no historical records exist.
15,000 Years Ago	Dume named Turaga of Metru Nui.
4,000 Years Ago	Kanohi Dragon attacks Metru Nui. Defeated by Toa Lhikan and his team.
3,000 Years Ago	Toa–Dark Hunter War. Dark Hunters defeated.
1,300 Years Ago	Six Toa Hagah are mutated into bestial Rahaga, but not before they steal the Mask of Light from the Brotherhood of Makuta.
1,050 Years Ago	Rahaga take refuge in Onu-Metru Archives.
1,001 Years Ago	Makuta, disguised as Turaga Dume, attempts to seize control of Metru Nui and is defeated by Toa Metru. The Great Cataclysm, a major earthquake, destroys much of city. Visorak spiders invade, defeated by Toa Hordika. Matoran and Toa Metru depart for island of Mata Nui, leaving real Dume and Rahaga to watch over city.
One Month Ago	Toa Nuva and Matoran return to Metru Nui.

THE INHABITANTS

THE TURAGA

The reborn Metru Nui is ruled by Turaga Dume. He has spent the past 1,000 years watching over his empty city, aided only by the Rahaga on their occasional visits. He is now assisted by the six Turaga who formerly ruled Mata Nui — Vakama, Nokama, Nuju, Whenua, Onewa, and Matau.

Thus far, relations have been strained between Dume and the other Turaga. While Dume was thrilled to see them and the Matoran return, he has never had to share rule before and it is a new experience. As crises mount, he finds himself growing short-tempered with the others. The six Mata Nui Turaga forged quite different, almost paternal, relationships with the Matoran, something Dume has a hard time understanding.

THE MATORAN

Six tribes of Matoran originated on Metru Nui, and later moved to the island of Mata Nui.

Ta-Matoran:	Affiliated with the element of fire. Formerly mask and tool makers, later lava farmers on Mata Nui.
Ko-Matoran:	Affiliated with the element of ice. Once the seers and scholars of Metru Nui, then trackers and trap builders on Mata Nui.
Le-Matoran:	Affiliated with the element of air. Masters of the transport system on Metru Nui, bird wranglers and hunters on Mata Nui.
Ga-Matoran:	Affiliated with the element of water. Students and teachers on Metru Nui, fish catchers and sailors on Mata Nui.
Po-Matoran:	Affiliated with the element of stone. Po-Matoran were renowned for their carving both on Metru Nui and on Mata Nui.
Onu-Matoran:	Affiliated with the element of earth. Primarily archivists on Metru Nui, and miners on Mata Nui.

The Matoran are faced with three interesting challenges in their newly rediscovered homeland. First, they must rebuild it, a massive undertaking. Second, the actions of Makuta left them with no memories of their life on Metru Nui, so they must relearn the technology. And finally, now that they are back on Metru Nui, it is possible for new Matoran to once again come into being (something that could not happen on Mata Nui). It remains to be seen how this tight-knit group of Matoran who have been through so much together will respond to newcomers.

CREATURES OF METRU NUI

LONGFANGS

Although many of the Rahi of Metru Nui emigrated to Mata Nui, some chose to remain. Among these were the beasts the Rahaga nicknamed "longfangs," large reptilian creatures who live in the narrow tunnel network beneath the Archives. Normally content to stay there in the past, the devastation of the earthquake and the subsequent flight of many small Rahi species forced them to come into the city searching for food. Although Dume wished the beasts to be trapped, the Rahaga refused, saying that the longfangs were now a part of the natural environment of the city.

Longfangs average seven feet in length, with short, powerful jaws lined with multiple rows of sharp teeth. Their preferred prey is stone rats, but they will pursue much larger creatures if they see the opportunity or are driven to it by hunger.

UPDATE

In addition to the Turaga's many other worries (see Chapter Four), there are now signs that the ground around the city's largest building is in upheaval. For some weeks, the area surrounding the Coliseum has been cracking, buckling, and in a few cases collapsing completely. The Turaga believe there must be a connection to the current crisis involving the Great Spirit Mata Nui. No doubt they are correct, but what can be done about it remains a grim mystery.

VOYA NUI

In appearance, it seems to be only an insignificant speck of land in a great blue sea — hardly worth the time spent looking at it, let alone a place worth visiting. In reality, Voya Nui has hidden a secret for 100,000 years, one it has only very recently divulged. Strangely, this has led to the future of the island and its residents being more uncertain than ever before.

GETTING THERE

Voya Nui can be reached by ship or by airship. However, due to the large amount of ice in the waters around the island, an approach from the north is the only safe method of reaching the island by sea.

Recent visitors, of course, have come via Toa canister. These one-person transport units are capable of moving through solid rock as if it were water and respond to the rider's thoughts. They are not built for a safe and comfortable ride, however, and common wisdom is that no one with less than the power of a Toa would survive their use.

THE LAND

Voya Nui is a harsh and brutal land, particularly in recent years. Those Matoran forced to make a life here have had to struggle each day simply to survive. This was not an accident. By being as inhospitable as possible, the island has discouraged casual visitors and those chasing its secret.

Surrounding the U-shaped coastline of Voya Nui is a ring of ice. Moving farther inland, a traveler encounters the "green belt," a circular band of lush jungle whose origin remains a mystery to the Matoran. Once past the green belt, the land turns rocky and barren. Dominating the center of the island is an active volcano, Mount Valmai.

What few in the known universe know is that the true importance of Voya Nui can be found only belowground. A hidden entrance leads to a 777-step staircase, which in turn leads to the chamber that holds the Mask of Life. Many guardians and challenges were placed here to prevent the mask from being taken by those with evil intent. For thousands of years, no one dared descend the stairs, until in recent days a team of Piraka and a team of Toa Inika made the journey. Amazingly, both groups survived the experience.

Voya Nui was once home to two villages, one named simply Voya Nui and the second named Mahri Nui. The land that held the latter broke off from the rest of the island and sank beneath the sea (see Chapter Eleven).

HISTORY

For most of its existence, Voya Nui was part of a much larger continent. Then the Great Cataclysm came, the same quake that wrecked the city of Metru Nui. The Voya Nui landmass broke off of its home continent and rocketed upward until it reached the point where it now floats, well to the north of its starting point. In the process, its ruler, Turaga Jovan, and many Matoran were killed.

One would have expected the island to continue to float away on the waves, but that did not happen. Instead, molten protodermis oozing from its core cooled instantly in the ocean waters, forming a labyrinthine chain of solid rock that extended from Voya Nui down below the surface and held it in place.

Now leaderless, the Matoran nevertheless adjusted in time to their new environment. The landmass of Voya Nui increased over the years, until there was room to build a coastal city, christened Mahri Nui. Then a second disaster struck — Mahri Nui sank beneath the sea, taking all of its residents with it. To this day, the Matoran of Voya Nui throw tools and other artifacts into the water at that spot as a memorial to their lost friends.

After that tragedy, life remained peaceful for many millennia. The Matoran dealt with drought, volcanic eruptions, and other natural disasters, scraping out a living from the rocky earth. Until very recently, none were aware that they shared the island with two members of the Order of Mata Nui, Axonn and Brutaka. These two had been assigned there ages ago to keep watch over the entryway to the Mask of Life's hiding place.

The situation began to unravel in the last month. First a Piraka named Vezon, then six others — Zaktan, Avak, Hakann, Thok, Reidak, and Vezok — invaded the island in search of the Mask of Life. They enslaved the Matoran, battled two teams of Toa, and came within inches of claiming the mask before finally being frustrated in their efforts. But they were not captured and continue to seek the mask, although their physical forms have been affected by mutagenic seawater. It is doubtful even they know just what changes await them.

In the aftermath of this struggle, the Toa Inika found, and lost, the mask and are now on their way to Mahri Nui in pursuit of it. Their fellow heroes, the Toa Nuva, have departed the island on a mission of their own. Brutaka has been exiled, leaving only Axonn and the Matoran on the island. How much longer they remain there will depend on what success the Toa Inika find in the ocean depths.

THE INHABITANTS

THE MATORAN

Representatives of the six major tribes of Matoran can all be found here. However, these Matoran are not native to this land. They were shipped here from the realm of Karzahni (see Chapter Two) after that domain's ruler botched the job of "repairing" them. As a result, these Matoran are smaller and weaker than most. They are well armed, though, thanks to Karzahni's guilt over what he did to them.

The Matoran of Voya Nui have done an excellent job of governing themselves, seeing to their own needs and defenses, all without the aid of a Turaga or Toa. In some ways, the series of disasters they have been through has been a benefit. More than almost any other Matoran, they will be able to answer the call when the final battles against the darkness begin.

ΛＸＯ∩∩

Axonn was at one time one of the greatest warriors in the BIONICLE universe. Whole cities fell before his axe, and his name sent shudders of fear through the inhabitants of the far southern lands. Left to himself, he might well have continued on this path until he ran out of lands to conquer or was defeated by someone more powerful.

The Order of Mata Nui offered him a better way. We showed him how he could use his great abilities in the service of something greater than himself. Giving up his dreams of empire, he became a trusted member of our organization. After a series of adventures in our service, he was assigned to Voya Nui to guard the Mask of Life. This he did long and well, even when his duty required that he do battle with his best friend.

Axonn remains on Voya Nui to this day, watching over the Matoran who live there and preparing for the potentially cataclysmic events to come. May the Great Spirit Mata Nui grant him strength to do what he must.

BRUTAKA

Like Axonn, Brutaka was a powerful and accomplished being when first recruited for the Order. Where Axonn was a warrior, Brutaka was more a scholar, though one versed in the art of the sword. His intelligence and ability to analyze facts quickly were seen as a good combination with Axonn's raw power.

Unfortunately, these traits betrayed him. When the Great Spirit Mata Nui was plunged into endless sleep, Brutaka came to the conclusion that he had

either died or else abandoned this universe. Over time, he lost all faith, and so was ripe to be tempted by dreams of power. When the Piraka came to Voya Nui, he allied himself with them, intending to let them get the Mask of Life and then take it away from them.

In the end, Axonn defeated Brutaka and he was spirited away to serve out eternity in the Pit. But there is reason to fear that even in that dismal place, Brutaka's ambitions will lead him astray.

CREATURES OF VOYA NUI

SAND SCREAMER

Of the Rahi who have managed to survive on Voya Nui, few are as mysterious as the beast known as the sand screamer. Although it is classified as a Rahi, no one is truly sure whether this is an animal or some other type of being. It has been heard among the barren terrain of the island, screaming in the middle of the night as if in agony — but it has never been seen. Tracks sighted by Matoran disappear within a matter of seconds. Signs are most often found around the dead bodies of larger beasts, suggesting that whatever the sand screamer is, it is potentially dangerous.

UPDATE

With the defeat of the Piraka and Brutaka, peace has returned to Voya Nui. Axonn is now struggling to convince the Matoran to stay on the island and wait to find out what the Toa Inika discover in their quest for the Mask of Life. Many of the villagers, led by Garan, wish to explore beneath the waves to discover if, by some miracle, Mahri Nui still exists.

MATA NUI

To those Matoran who lived and worked on the island of Mata Nui for over 1,000 years, it seemed a paradise. Despite the presence of dangerous Rahi beasts and the unpredictability of the weather, Matoran thrived amid the lush jungles, sparkling rivers, snowcapped peaks, and vast, barren plains. Little did they realize that no one was ever meant to live on this island, or the danger they faced by doing so.

The island named after the Great Spirit Mata Nui was located in the world above our own. It is a place the Matoran fled to in a time of desperation, and where they were then forced to remain. Now they have finally abandoned the island and returned to their true home, Metru Nui.

GETTING THERE

Mata Nui can be reached by land through a myriad of tunnels leading up from Metru Nui. These tunnels were originally built to allow the Bohrok swarms access to the island. (The Bohrok currently rest in nests under Mata Nui and Metru Nui, awaiting a signal to awaken. Once they have received it, they will proceed to Mata Nui to cleanse it of all rocks, trees, rivers, etc., and reduce it again to the barren place it once was. A previous, ill-timed attempt to do this was defeated by Toa Tahu and his team.)

Mata Nui can also be reached by sea from the island of Voya Nui. However, the inhabitants of that island do not know of the existence of Mata Nui and so have never attempted to make the journey.

THE LAND

Mata Nui is divided into six zones, which can be told apart by both terrain and climate. These are:

Ko-Wahi: An icy region, known for its snowfalls and avalanches. Site of Mount Ihu, highest point on the island.

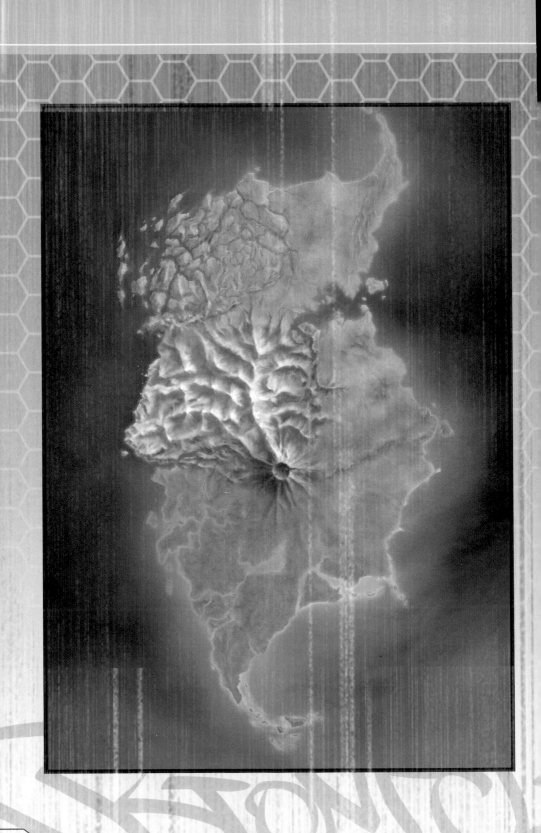

Po-Wahi: A barren, rocky wasteland.

Le-Wahi: A region of thick, green jungle and fetid swamps.

Ta-Wahi: A hot, volcanic region, site of the Mangai volcano.

Ga-Wahi: Region in northeastern Mata Nui dominated by the waters of Naho Bay.

Onu-Wahi: A largely barren region riddled with underground, Matoran-made tunnels.

Each of the wahi was home to a koro, or village, built by the Matoran and their Turaga leaders. The Matoran adapted well to their new surroundings, making use of natural terrain for defense as well as training some of the Rahi beasts who had traveled to the island from below.

HISTORY

As stated in Chapter Three, the Matoran of Metru Nui were forced to relocate to Mata Nui after their city was largely destroyed by an attack by Makuta, an earthquake, and a subsequent invasion by Visorak spiders. Using parts of the airships that carried them to the island, the Matoran and their Turaga constructed villages, along with parts of a temple called Kini-Nui, shrines to legendary Toa, and an observatory. Due to the efforts of Makuta, the Matoran did not remember their previous existence on Metru Nui. However, the Turaga did, and never stopped dreaming of returning to their homeland.

The Matoran enjoyed a single year of peace on Mata Nui. Then Makuta attacked again, this time using Rahi beasts controlled by infected Kanohi masks. At first, it seemed strange that Makuta did not unleash all his power to either enslave or destroy the Matoran. Then it became obvious that all he was really trying to do was keep the Matoran penned in their villages, scared, and far away from Metru Nui.

The constant attacks made travel between the koro difficult and dangerous. But the Matoran did not back down. They formed defense forces — the Ta-Koro Guard, the Ussalry in Onu-Koro, the Gukko Bird Force in Le-Koro — to protect themselves. And they anxiously awaited the coming of Toa, legendary figures whom the Turaga claimed would save them from Makuta.

Of course, the Toa did eventually arrive and were later joined by a seventh Toa, Takanuva, Toa of Light. Led by Tahu, Toa of Fire, the team defeated Makuta's Rahi, the invasions of the Bohrok and Bohrok-Kal, and the evil Rahkshi. Finally, Takanuva defeated Makuta himself and opened the way for the Matoran to return to Metru Nui at last.

Note: There is some question whether Makuta was actually defeated by Takanuva or simply let the Toa think they had won. Recent events on Voya Nui hint that the Master of Shadows is not dead but still trying to carry out some grand scheme involving the Kanohi Mask of Life.

THE INHABITANTS

THE TOA

Much has already been written about Tahu, Gali, Pohatu, Onua, Lewa, and Kopaka, so there is little need to repeat their records of achievement. But for those Order of Mata Nui members who may not be as familiar with history as they should be, a brief summary:

Unlike all other Toa known to us, Tahu and his team were never Matoran and never "transformed" into Toa. They came into being as heroes, complete with elemental powers and Masks of Power. After a number of adventures in the place Matoran call "the world that feeds the world," they were chosen to take on the role of the Great Spirit's protectors. Placed in Toa transport canisters, they waited for the day that the Great Spirit Mata Nui might fall — if this happened, their task would be to reawaken him.

When the Great Spirit was struck down by Makuta, the Toa's canisters were launched into the world above. The plan was for them to make landfall on the island of Mata Nui and then journey down to Metru Nui to begin their mission. But something went wrong. The canisters malfunctioned and the Toa floated in stasis in the waters around Mata Nui for 1,000 years.

By the time they reached the island, they discovered that Matoran had built a civilization there and Makuta had firm control of the underground. Many battles would have to be fought before they could even begin their job of freeing the Great Spirit from endless sleep.

THE MATORAN

Six tribes of Matoran lived on Mata Nui, the same villagers who had once inhabited Metru Nui. It was, in some ways, a blessing that they did not remember their life before, for the island was quite different from their home. Where the various metru of Metru Nui could work together, the koro of Mata Nui were largely isolated. The Matoran were forced to become self sufficient hunters, and fighters, builders, without the luxury of relying on Toa to protect them. As a result, they are among the most unique Matoran in the universe — far more than just workers, they are a strong people willing and able to fight against the darkness.

THE TURAGA

The six Turaga of Mata Nui — Vakama, Nokama, Whenua, Onewa, Matau, and Nuju — were briefly heroes themselves. They served as the Toa Metru in Metru Nui, fighting against Makuta and the Visorak hordes and largely winning. While they could not save the city, they did save the Matoran inhabitants and get them to safety on Mata Nui.

For 1,000 years, they watched over the Matoran and kept the secret of Metru Nui from them. It was only after the city was rediscovered that they shared the tales of all that had taken place there. Perhaps it might have been better for everyone if they had spoken up earlier — but it is not for us to question destiny, as decreed by the Great Spirit Mata Nui.

CHAPTER FIVE

CREATURES OF MATA NUI

Those with an interest in the various wildlife of Mata Nui are instructed to read the tablets prepared by the Rahaga and collected as Rahi Beasts in the Order's library. There is, however, one creature about which they could know nothing, so we include it here.

MANA KO

These fierce, monstrous beasts are known in Matoran legend as the ultimate guardian of Makuta's lair beneath Mata Nui. Their bodies are rectangular and blocky, with eyes perched high in a red and yellow head. The Mana Ko are capable of firing explosive blasts of devastating power, which they will gladly do at anything that moves. What no one realizes — not even the Brotherhood of Makuta — is that the Mana Ko are loyal to the Order of Mata Nui. We allow them to serve the Brotherhood for as long as it suits our purposes and they relay any information they learn back to us. They have done an excellent job keeping outsiders away from Brotherhood weapons and equipment, things that we don't want anyone else having, either. But the day will come when we summon the Mana Ko back to stand beside us in the final battle.

UPDATE

Since the Matoran's return to Metru Nui, the island of Mata Nui is now abandoned. It is vitally important that neither they nor anyone else be allowed to take up residence there! Also, a way must be found to unleash the Bohrok once again so that the island can be made to look as it once did. The Great Spirit Mata Nui will expect nothing less on the day of his reawakening.

DAXIA

It may seem strange to devote a chapter to the island base of the Order of Mata Nui, considering how familiar it is to all those who are reading this. But knowledge — complete knowledge — is always of use. The day may come when, Mata Nui forbid, our Order may be decimated and only a few of our members survive. If that is ever the case, this record may help them to rebuild.

The island of Daxia has been the homeland of the Order since the beginning of time. It was here that the Toa Mata — Tahu, Gali, Pohatu, Onua, Lewa, and Kopaka — first walked. It was here that plans were first made to deceive the evil Makuta and so bring about the creation of the Toa Metru in Metru Nui. And it is here that, if need be, we will fight the final battle to save the Great Spirit and his works.

THE LAND

Mountainous and beautiful, Daxia is a paradise. More importantly, it is a paradise that can be easily defended from behind the walls of our fortress. It is the first and the largest Order of Mata Nui base, and all our members have standing orders to fall back to this island in the event their position is overrun.

A stranger visiting Daxia would probably not agree that it is an attractive place to settle. There are no obvious sources of fresh water, the climate is blisteringly hot year-round, and the wildlife can be quite ferocious. But for those who get to know the island well, there are treasures to be found. Tiny streams trickle down the mountains and turn into underground lakes. The high temperatures produce plant life not found anywhere else in the universe. And the local creatures primarily target each other, unless there is an intruder to the island upon whom to feast.

HISTORY

The first sunlight had just barely illuminated this universe when the Great Beings realized there was a need for our organization. The Toa would be the public face of the Great Spirit Mata Nui's will, serving and protecting the Matoran workers and so earning their trust. But the importance of maintaining that trust and their image as heroes meant there would be some jobs Toa could not do and some they could know nothing about. Another body was required, one dedicated solely to the Great Spirit, with no other loyalties or allegiances to get in the way. That body became the Order of Mata Nui.

The first recruits for the Order came from among the ranks of those who oversaw the building of Karzahni and Artakha, well before the coming of any Toa. Those original members chose Daxia as the site of the Order's fortress. They built it themselves, stone by stone, with no help from Matoran or any others. When it was finished, they made a vow — to keep the Order, its membership, and the location of Daxia a secret. Breaking that vow, except in extreme circumstances, would be punishable by death.

In its time, the Order has acted only when it had to and when the Toa could not. Plans of the Dark Hunters, the League of Six Kingdoms, the Brotherhood of Makuta, and others have been checked in part by our operatives. Regrettably, some of our actions have led to the deaths of Toa or Matoran, something that could not be avoided if we were to maintain the anonymity that is our greatest strength. In the end, though we might wish it otherwise, saving the lives of even Toa cannot be more important than the interests of the Great Spirit Mata Nui.

Over the millennia, our fortress has been upgraded to feature the very latest technology and weaponry. Although we are confident that no enemy is aware of our location, it makes no sense to stake our lives and futures on it. An attempt at invasion would be met with devastating power, sufficient to destroy the island and everything on it. We will leave no secrets behind for anyone else to exploit.

Today, the Order of Mata Nui is hundreds strong, with agents scattered across the universe. Although we are outnumbered by our foes, we make up for that with sheer power. While Brotherhood of Makuta members could likely stand up to an Order attack, those who serve them would be scattered to the winds by even one blow from one of our operatives. Or so we believe . . .

Of course, no organization can hope to know only victory. Most recently, we were forced to confront the betrayal of one of our own, Brutaka. He and his teammate, Axonn, had been stationed on Voya Nui for many thousands of years. Somewhere along the way, Brutaka lost faith in the Great Spirit. When the Piraka came to the island in search of the Mask of Life, he allied with them. Axonn was forced into combat with his friend and managed to defeat Brutaka. Botar was then dispatched from Daxia to transport the fallen Order member to the Pit, where we are confident he will remain forever.

THE INHABITANTS

Other than members of the Order, no intelligent beings dwell on Daxia. We have no workers, no servants, no slaves, but see to our own needs. It is better and safer that way for all concerned. Our members come from numerous species, each bringing unique talents and abilities as well as a passionate commitment to the Order's mission.

That commitment is essential. Those who are recruited into the Order surrender their lives and their freedom in the cause of the Great Spirit. They cannot look forward to a life of ease in the future, or even contemplate leaving the Order to pursue another life path. It is for this reason that we test potential members so thoroughly (and in secret) before making them an offer. Even then, they are not given a clear picture of what they will be doing or who they will be joining. Only when we are certain they will serve with honor do we reveal the truth to them. Thus far, no one has ever rejected an offer of membership.

We have certain other requirements as well when seeking new members. We will not recruit Toa, Turaga, or Matoran, for they have their own roles to play in the universe quite apart from ours. Ex–Dark Hunters or former servants of the Brotherhood of Makuta are also not welcome in our ranks.

As proven by the incident with Brutaka, our recruiting methods are not infallible. We have had members betray our ideals in the past, and may again in the future. At such times, we turn to Botar. A member of a savage race of the southern islands, Botar sees the world in terms of pure good and pure evil. He lives for his job, which is to take those who are deemed beyond redemption to eternal imprisonment in the Pit. Although not physically more powerful than other Order members, his single-minded devotion to justice and punishment, total unwillingness to compromise, and long record of success makes even

those members who are loyal a bit afraid. The mere mention of his name is enough to make most potential traitors to the cause think twice. For those who do not, Botar teleports to their side and spirits them away to the abyss from which no one ever returns.

CREATURES OF DAXIA

SHALLOWS CAT

One of the strangest creatures to be found on Daxia is the shallows cat, a menace in past years even to some unwary Order members. Those walking along the shoreline may be surprised to see a sleek, beautiful creature vaguely resembling a Muaka cat emerge from the surf. It makes no threatening gestures, but simply stretches out on the sand to rest. So harmless does the shallows cat appear that one may be tempted to approach and befriend it. All who have tried have found themselves dragged into the shallows, drowned, and devoured. Like the Order of Mata Nui itself, the shallows cat keeps its true power hidden until the time is right to strike.

UPDATE

It would be comforting to think that our future will unfold much like our past, but we would be fools to believe it to be so. Even now, our enemies are massing. The Dark Hunters continue to war with the Brotherhood, while the struggle for the Mask of Life goes on beneath the waves. New and largely unknown factors like Karzahni pose a threat as well. The Order must be ever watchful and prepared for the day we must step out of the shadows and fight in the light.

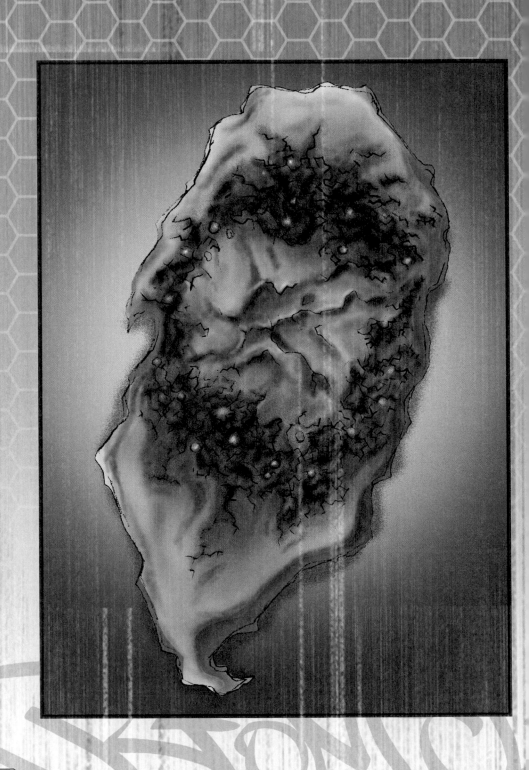

CHAPTER SEVEN

XIA

Xia is unlike any other island in this atlas. Where places like Zakaz, Destral, and Odina discourage visitors, Xia is more than happy to have you come — provided you are there to do business. And the business of Xia is death for those of other lands.

The island is known for three things:

- As an arsenal for the universe, from at least one warring faction on Zahaz to the Brotherhood of Makuta itself.
- As a dumping ground for the problems of other islands.
- As the native land of Roodaka, former queen of the Visorak horde and still a major figure in the Brotherhood of Makuta–Dark Hunter War.

Be prepared — Xia is a land dominated by greed. The greatest crime in their code is to make a deal that does not turn a profit. Doing so leads to immediate execution, or worse — a second visit to the Mountain.

GETTING THERE

The inhabitants of Xia are determined to make it easy for anyone to visit their island and buy their deadly wares. There are a number of sea routes available, patrolled by craft from Xia to make sure no sea raiders, Frostelus, or other menaces interfere with visiting ships. In fact, Xia recently tested one of its items by blasting a nearby island into dust so that it would not block an approach to their own. Fortunately, no intelligent species was living on the island at the time, but a number of rare types of Rahi beast were wiped out in the process.

Xia has an excellent port system as well as areas for airship landings. It is located within easy sailing distance of the city of Metru Nui — simply travel through the main southern sea gate and turn sharply east, staying close to the Great Barrier. Xia is easily visible from a kio away, and it is impossible to be mistaken for any other island.

THE LAND

The island of Xia is dominated by a rocky peak called simply "the Mountain" by residents. All around the peak — literally covering every inch of available space — are forges, factories, warehouses, and docks. The one thing you will not see is homes or shelters. Workers on this island sleep near their posts, in case a sudden order requires them to return to their labors immediately.

Environmentally, the island is a disaster. The air is black with soot and dust, and fresh water is nonexistent. The only source of water is a thin, dirty stream that winds around the Mountain, passing through countless factories on its way. Clean air is said to exist at the top of the peak, but since virtually no one cares to visit there more than once, it serves rather as a tease than a refuge from the pollution below.

HISTORY

Xia was, at one time, the northernmost island ruled by Pridak, a member of the League of Six Kingdoms. Given its abundance of natural resources and the industriousness of its people, Pridak ordered that it be the center of weapons production for his realm. Factories and forges were rapidly built and the inhabitants were put to work creating new and better war machines.

Pridak was eventually banished to the Pit, along with the rulers of the other kingdoms, and his realm broken up. But Xia went on working, producing weapons for whoever wanted to buy them. Their customers eventually included the Brotherhood of Makuta and the Dark Hunters. (Of course, the Dark Hunters never buy when they can steal, and they did in fact steal the prototypes for zamor launchers from another client of Xia. Attempts to hunt down the thieves were unsuccessful, but for a time the Dark Hunters were not welcome on the island.)

Xia has also served as a receptacle for things other islands did not want. After the defeat of the Kanohi Dragon by Toa Lhikan and his team, the beast was

brought here. It disappeared shortly afterward, but rumor has it that it is being studied in hopes of artificially reproducing its power.

Today, Xia's main customer is the Brotherhood. During the Visorak invasion of Metru Nui and other islands, Xia provided the catapults and other war machines used by the spiders. After the defeat of the Visorak by the Toa Metru, Roodaka returned here to heal her wounds and make plans for the future. It's said she even made a second trip up the Mountain to reaffirm her power and cunning.

THE INHABITANTS

The population of Xia is called the Vortixx. They are tall, lean, powerful beings, all in black armor. The society is dominated by females, and they are the only Vortixx allowed to ever leave the island. Males labor in the dirtiest and most dangerous jobs while females serve as overseers and weapons designers.

Every Vortixx is required at a certain time in their life to undergo a rite of passage. A male and a female climb the Mountain together. If they make it to the top and back, they are honored and given better working conditions.

But true praise is reserved for those cases where there is only one survivor, for that one has proven he or she has the ruthlessness required to survive.

For those who have had dealings with Roodaka in the past, it may come as a surprise that the Vortixx have no interest in conquest. They much prefer building weapons and letting others take the risks involved with battle. The Vortixx couldn't care less who wins or loses, or who reigns, as long as they get paid.

CREATURES OF XIA

THE MOUNTAIN

It might sound strange to list a rocky peak as a creature, but it is the closest thing to "wildlife" that exists on Xia. Outside of a few insects, no Rahi can live there. Those seabirds that migrate from other islands usually die from the pollution before they can finish making a nest among the smokestacks.

Although it looks like any other natural landmark, the Mountain is in fact sentient — meaning it is able to feel, if not necessarily think or plan. It can tell when Vortixx are climbing its slopes and it responds by attempting to consume them. Great crevices suddenly appear in the rock face and the next thing anyone knows, there is one less Vortixx in the universe.

The Mountain's nature was first discovered tens of thousands of years ago. A small group of Vortixx insisted that the Mountain should be fully explored, if only to provide a new challenge and a chance for discovery. Others argued that only bad things could come from this — maybe it was volcanic, or strange creatures lived on the Mountain. The supporters of exploration disagreed, in part because they felt confident they would escape any harm unscathed, and the only damage done would be to those who worked too near the slopes.

And so they shouted long and loud about the need to take risks, about the potential benefits of exploration, and displayed their bravery and resolve for all to see. Eventually, their opponents grew tired of fighting and allowed them to do what they wanted to do. Boldly, the small group of Vortixx started up the Mountain, ready to change the world . . . and were promptly eaten.

After that, the Vortixx avoided the Mountain for many years. Finally, someone decided that it really did take something akin to bravery to ignore people who knew better than you and march off to your potential doom out of sheer stubbornness. Doing so became the mark of a true Vortixx, the one risk to life and limb they allowed themselves to take, and the ritual continues to this day.

UPDATE

A rumor recently flashed through the streets of Xia — the League of Six Kingdoms was about to return to power. Even without confirmation, factories increased their production of every kind of weapon. If the Barraki were to come back, after all, massive destruction could be expected to follow.

Meanwhile, business remains brisk as both the Dark Hunters and the Brotherhood stock up on equipment for their ongoing conflict. Roodaka has brokered deals with both sides, and this has put her in line for rule of Xia. Whether she would continue the Vortixx policy of being peaceful suppliers of arms is unknown — based on her past, it would seem likely she would mobilize the population and attempt to conquer.

ODINA

The leader of the Dark Hunters, known only as the Shadowed One, flatters himself in thinking that he has kept the location of Odina concealed from the world. If he knew the Order of Mata Nui existed, he would realize that very little is concealed from us. We have known for centuries that Odina is the island headquarters of the dangerous and deadly organization known as the Dark Hunters. We allow it to continue to exist because it suits our purposes to do so. The Dark Hunters, for those unfamiliar with the name, are a group of mercenaries who will do anything for the right price. In their time, they have battled Toa, unleashed monstrous Rahi on defenseless cities, kidnapped Turaga, stolen artifacts, and even seized control of entire islands. For years, they were used by the Brotherhood of Makuta to strike at their foes. Even now, no Toa is truly safe as long as they exist.

Why the Shadowed One chose Odina for a base for the Dark Hunters is easy to see. It is well away from any normal trade routes. Its high cliffs make it extremely defensible. And with so few neighboring islands, no one will ever hear or see the terrible things that go on there.

GETTING THERE

Don't. We cannot state it any more simply than that. Why? Three reasons:

- Odina is home to one of the worst collections of thieves, killers, maniacs, and would-be tyrants in the universe — and they value their privacy.

- It is heavily defended. By the time you punch your way through those defenses, whatever or whoever you have gone there to get will have been spirited off the island.

- The Dark Hunters have been at war with the Brotherhood of Makuta for over 1,000 years, dating back to a dispute between the Shadowed One and the Makuta of Metru Nui. Striking at them will aid the Brotherhood, something it is not in our interest to do. Let the Shadowed One go on thinking his base is a secret, until we see fit to reveal the truth to him.

THE LAND

Odina is most remarkable for its cliffs. They rise hundreds of feet in the air on every side of the island, huge monoliths of black stone that cut the island's interior off from the outside world. Only one pathway leads from the upper plateau down to the coast, emerging at a spot called Nidhiki Beach. (It is so named because it was on this strip of sand that the traitorous Toa Nidhiki was transformed into a monstrous insectoid being, by order of the Shadowed One.)

The only other feature of significance on the island is the Dark Hunter fortress and training ground. Covering most of the southern half of the island, it is as close to impregnable as its builders could make it. Over time, even the Brotherhood of Makuta's strongholds have been invaded and robbed — this has never happened on Odina.

The secrets of its builders went to the grave with them, but it is known that the stone of the fortress's inner hallways has some unusual properties. Apparently, the entire configuration of the building can be changed by the Shadowed One's thoughts, allowing him to herd intruders wherever he wants them to go. The structure is also loaded with traps, dead ends (accent on dead), and prisons for those foolish enough to be caught and lucky enough to survive the experience.

The courtyard of the fortress serves as a training area where Dark Hunters are taught to kidnap, to steal, and to eliminate their enemies. There is no mock combat on Odina. All fights, even training exercises, are to the death, unless the Shadowed One wishes it otherwise.

HISTORY

The island of Odina was discovered by the Shadowed One and a being nicknamed "Ancient," a fellow native of the Shadowed One's homeland. In the wake of a civil war there, the two had hit upon the idea of offering their services to others in return for profit or power. From there, it was a short leap to the idea of hiring others to serve under them and take on missions, turning over any reward they received to the organization.

Being more ambitious and determined, the Shadowed One eventually took over sole leadership of the organization. But the Dark Hunters needed a secure base and a place to train new recruits. For the reasons stated above, Odina proved to be ideal. The Shadowed One and Ancient promptly scared off or killed the native population and made the island their own.

Over the millennia, countless plans have been hatched on this island that resulted in acts of both great daring and great evil. Virtually every artifact of importance, from the Makoki stones to the Mask of Life, has at one time or another been possessed by or coveted by the Dark Hunters. At any time of the day or night, boats or airships can be seen coming and going from Odina, ferrying agents to and from their missions.

Only once in all that time has the security of Odina ever truly been at risk. After the Dark Hunters' defeat in their war with the Toa, the heroes could have chosen to force the location of the island from their prisoners. Instead, in an effort to retrieve the Makoki stones (whose true importance they did not even know), the Toa made a deal with the Shadowed One that allowed the captured Dark Hunters to return to their base. No one on either side believed it would be the last confrontation between the two.

Today, Odina is the headquarters for the war against the Brotherhood. Although the Shadowed One is confident that his enemies will not attempt to storm his fortress, he is not aware of the fact there is a spy in his midst. The Xia native named Roodaka has been working for both sides in the conflict and will gladly sell out the Dark Hunters if the price is right.

THE INHABITANTS

Unlike Xia or the Matoran-held islands, the population of Odina is extremely varied. Dark Hunters come from many species, and usually fall into one of five groups:

Criminal Nature: Some Dark Hunters are simply evil, violent, or immoral, and enjoy destruction for the sake of destruction.

Social Outcasts: Those who have been shunned because of their appearance or behavior and believe they have nowhere else to go are easily recruited into the Dark Hunters' ranks.

All Brawn, No Brains: Some members only have one talent — breaking things — and are happy to put it to use in return for food and shelter.

The Victims: Those who, through trickery or blackmail or some other means, have been forced into joining the organization or made to believe they cannot leave.

The Cunning: A small group with a short life expectancy, these are the members who remain because they dream of one day overthrowing the Shadowed One and taking over the Dark Hunters.

United in their fear of their leader, their disconnection from normal society, and their talent for violence, the Dark Hunters are a threat that we will one day have to deal with severely.

CREATURES OF ODINA

CLIFF SCREECHER

One of the few native species to survive Odina's occupation by the Dark Hunters, the cliff screecher has a rich mythology attached to it. The batlike creature was said by Odina's natives to be incapable of dying, because its spirit was housed somewhere other than its body. Whether there is any truth to that or not, the facts about the cliff screecher are just as disturbing. When hungry or irritable, it will attack anything attempting to scale its cliffs, preceding its dive with the loud screech that gave it its name. After knocking its victim off the rock, it will actually swoop down, catch its prey, and then return it to the cliff face — only to knock it off again. It will continue to do this until its prey dies from shock and fear. Not the most efficient way to hunt, but evidently effective and certainly cruel.

UPDATE

Events have been changing rapidly on Odina. The Shadowed One's agent off the shores of Voya Nui has informed him that the Toa Inika found and lost the Mask of Life, and the six Piraka are nowhere to be seen. The Shadowed One now faces the most difficult decision of his career: whether or not to split his forces and make an all-out effort to claim the mask, at the risk of leaving the Dark Hunters vulnerable to an attack by the Brotherhood of Makuta. Anticipating this, we are already taking steps to block any efforts he may make and give the Toa Inika time to recover the mask.

ZAKAZ

Once a green and lush land, Zakaz is now a monument to senseless destruction. In ancient times, it was home to many beautiful and advanced cities, a sophisticated transportation network, and abundant resources. Now it is known only for its rubble and ruins, its constant warfare, and the perpetual haze of black smoke from countless fires.

It would be easy to blame the inhabitants of Zakaz for destroying their land. But the truth is far darker and far more tragic, and we of the Order of Mata Nui must share some of the responsibility. We could have stopped this from happening, but we did not act, instead placing our trust in those who live only to betray.

GETTING THERE

Travel to Zakaz is forbidden, by order of the Brotherhood of Makuta (one of the few matters upon which we agree with them). Those determined to get there will find it to lie just south of the realm of Karzahni, several days' travel away from Metru Nui. If traveling by sea, be advised there are no working ports left on Zakaz. Travel by airship is more practical; however, robotic nektann are placed at key points all over the island to blast any unauthorized airships out of the sky. Go there at your own risk.

THE LAND

The most obvious way to begin this description is to ask, "What land?" Where once crops grew, it is now a barren and blasted landscape. Trees have been felled and rocks mined to build fortresses, which are blown to pieces in a matter of days or weeks. Resources like water and food are scarce. Those foolish enough to travel too close to the jagged coastline often wind up with their boats plundered and then sunk.

Given all that, the reader might wonder why the population doesn't try to flee. Why stay in such a war-torn place? In short, the answer is that they aren't wanted anywhere else, and for good reason (see "Inhabitants"). A few attempts to invade and conquer other islands by the residents of Zakaz were beaten back by Toa. So there they stay, fighting and dying over piles of rock and sand.

HISTORY

Some 75,000 years ago, Zakaz was a thriving island. While its natives, the Skakdi, were never the friendliest or the most trustworthy, they generally managed to live in peace among themselves and with their neighbors.

All that changed with the coming of a Brotherhood of Makuta member whose name has been lost to time. The Brotherhood claimed at the time that he was a renegade, and they were believed, but now it seems more likely he was there under orders. He looked at the Skakdi and saw a potential army — and we of the Order did not realize what was about to take place.

Exactly what happened next is unclear, but the Brotherhood member began tampering with the natural order on Zakaz. As years passed, the Skakdi exhibited vision powers, like heat vision, impact vision, and more. They also developed elemental powers, which they could use only if working together. No doubt the Brotherhood believed these abilities would make them better fighters in a future war.

The Brotherhood member left the island, planning to return later and leaving Visorak spiders to keep an eye on things. The spiders didn't enjoy a long stay. The Skakdi rose up and wiped them out, then turned on each other. With the new powers at their command, every minor dispute turned into a battle, and every battle into full-scale destruction. Empires came into being in a matter of days and were crushed just as quickly. Government and laws broke down and chaos swept the island. By the time the Brotherhood member returned to check up on his experiment, half the population was warring with the other half.

The result of all this was that the Brotherhood never did recruit the Skakdi in any large numbers. They were regarded as too violent and too unstable ever to serve anyone for long. Instead, the island was quarantined, with only Dark Hunters being brave enough to risk visiting the place.

THE INHABITANTS

It would be interesting to know how the Skakdi might have turned out had things been different. If Zakaz had more resources, if the Brotherhood had not used it as a living laboratory, if the Skakdi were a little less brutal by nature . . . so many ifs.

The Skakdi are tall, powerful beings with hideous faces that seem to be set in a permanent, bestial smile. An organic "spine" extends from the back of the head down the back of the arms, and those arms end in claws. All Skakdi have some sort of vision-based power, and some have additional abilities as well. Just as many others are damaged in some way, mad, or otherwise warped by the Brotherhood's "gifts."

The Skakdi are, as a rule, warlike, brutal, traitorous, and violent — and those are their nicer qualities. Their six most infamous examples became Dark Hunters and later betrayed that group, banding together under the name Piraka. Every settlement, from the smallest village to the largest city, is at war on Zakaz, which explains why so few are left standing. Those Skakdi who have survived — and that is a surprisingly large number — live among the ruins. A Skakdi who commands a place where three or more stones are still stacked together is considered a power to be reckoned with.

Most Skakdi live out their lives and perish on Zakaz. Death is the only way off the island, unless one is lucky enough to be recruited by the Dark Hunters. Their power makes them attractive as troops or enforcers, but their reputation for treachery means they can be hired only at great risk.

CREATURES OF ZAKAZ

TAHTORAK

Ages ago, the massive creatures known as Tahtorak lived in herds that spanned hundreds of kios. Over time, the land bridges they crossed disintegrated, stranding them wherever they happened to be. A large number ended up on Zakaz, serving as mounts for the Skakdi.

Tahtorak are reptilian creatures who average forty feet in height and are more than capable of destroying an entire city when in a bad mood. They are surprisingly intelligent beasts, and for a time, it was a mystery why they would serve the Skakdi rather than crush them. A dying Tahtorak later revealed to an Order of Mata Nui member that the creatures did plan on wiping out the Skakdi eventually, but were willing to wait for the moment it would be most satisfying. Tahtorak are, it seems, very patient beasts.

SPINE SLUGS

Harmless, if revolting, creatures, spine slugs are parasites that attach themselves to the organic tissue making up Skakdi spines. They seem to somehow gain nourishment from a Skakdi's battle rage, in a way we have not yet discovered. Some believe they actually feed that rage in some way so that the Skakdi will continue to fight and thus provide more nourishment. If the spine slugs are connected to the Skakdi's violent tempers, it hardly matters, because the Skakdi would never admit it or do anything about it — it might cost them their edge in combat.

CHAPTER NINE

UPDATE

A few developments of interest on Zakaz:

- The central water source on the island has been declared a free zone. The various warring factions can travel there and back in peace, and most make an effort to avoid encountering each other. How long this fragile agreement will last is anyone's guess.

- Dark Hunter watercraft have been spotted in the waters around Zakaz. We suspect that the Dark Hunters believe the Piraka will return here with the Mask of Life, and so they are planning an ambush.

- A ship from Xia landed on the southern coast one week ago, unloaded some cargo onto the sand, and left. The cargo later disappeared. It may be that one of the faction leaders succeeded in contacting the Vortixx and made a deal for weapons and equipment. If that's the case, the balance of power may shift rapidly on Zakaz.

CHAPTER TEN

DESTRAL

Once, this island was a symbol of justice, truth, and loyalty. But history has blackened its name, until the sight of the barren plain and the harsh, forbidding fortress that rests upon it is enough to sicken any honorable being.

Destral is the site of one of the largest of the Brotherhood of Makuta fortresses. It is the headquarters in their war with the Dark Hunters, as well as their continuing criminal acts against the universe as a whole. So impregnable is this fortress that even members of our own Order of Mata Nui shudder at the thought of trying to capture it. But as long as it stands, it represents our failure to protect all who live from these brutal, ruthless traitors.

GETTING THERE

The Brotherhood makes no effort to erect barriers at sea or in the air to prevent visitors (or invaders) from reaching this island. Enemies who never make it to its shores cannot be captured, interrogated, or experimented upon. To the Brotherhood of Makuta, this would seem an atrocious waste.

Exactly where Destral is located is another matter. As best as we can gather, the Brotherhood either has access to a far more powerful version of the Kanohi Olmak, the Mask of Dimensional Gates, or else to a wearer for the standard version who is simply able to take advantage of every last bit of its energy. Periodically, the entire island of Destral disappears, only to reappear somewhere else in the universe, making it the ultimate mobile base. Our agents who have seen this happen have told us that the island appears to pass through a massive dimensional gate at the time of its disappearance. If this is true, the Brotherhood has an incredibly potent weapon at their command. One can only wonder why they have not used it more often.

THE LAND

From the beginning, it was known that the Brotherhood required very little in the way of luxuries or resources. Their primary requirement was space for experiments and access to large amounts of energized protodermis, that mysterious substance known for its ability to transform . . . or destroy. They found both on Destral and built their first facility there.

Destral remains today as it was then, a largely barren region dominated by the Brotherhood's fortress. Although the island itself is easy to get to, once on the rocky shore, concealed weaponry and scores of cleverly hidden traps wait for the unwary. If there is a weakness in the Brotherhood's security, it is that it is somewhat easier to break out and escape the island than it is to break in.

An interesting side note is that the Brotherhood at one time attempted to export some of the living rock of Xia's Mountain to this island, hoping to use it for added security. The effort failed because the rock developed a taste for the Visorak spiders that prowl the fortress grounds.

The fortress itself is massive, with living quarters for the Brotherhood members, workshops, laboratories, armories, prison cells, interrogation chambers, and a library of forbidden knowledge. It is guarded at all times by Visorak, by the violent armored beings called Rahkshi, and by mechanical Exo-Toa armored suits.

HISTORY

Anyone reading this volume already knows the dark and treacherous history of the Brotherhood of Makuta, but for the sake of clarity, we will summarize it here. The Brotherhood was established 100,000 years ago, within a matter of days of our own Order. Their assigned task was a simple one: Using energized protodermis as their tool, create whatever was needed to maintain the good order of the universe and carry out the will of Mata Nui. While they did not bring

Matoran, Toa, or the other intelligent species into being, they were responsible for the creation of countless breeds of Rahi beast.

As time passed, their excellent work led to their being given more responsibility. They became a smaller, but more powerful, security force for the universe, supplementing the efforts of the Toa. When massive threats emerged, such as the rebellion of the League of Six Kingdoms, the Brotherhood had the authority to muster an army of Toa and other beings in response. Later, the outbreak of the Matoran civil war in Metru Nui led to the assignment of individual Brotherhood members to different regions. Their duty: Monitor the environment, protect the Matoran, and provide support and guidance to the Toa, while still carrying out their primary role of creating whatever was needed to keep the universe in order.

What no one realized was that the battle with the League had planted an idea in the mind of the Makuta assigned to Metru Nui. Perhaps it was possible, he reasoned, for the Great Spirit Mata Nui to be overthrown and replaced? And if so, who better suited to make the attempt than the Brotherhood itself?

What happened next remains unclear, even after all these centuries. How much of the successful attack made on the Great Spirit was planned, and how much accident, is a mystery. It is also uncertain whether the Makuta of Metru Nui recruited his fellow members before or after striking.

What is certain is that the Brotherhood began oppressing and enslaving Matoran and creating dangerous Rahi mutations to serve their organization. By the time their treachery was suspected, they had already assembled a massive army of Visorak spiders and mechanical Exo-Toa. Still, they managed to keep their true plans a secret for centuries.

The crisis came a little over 1,000 years ago in Metru Nui. Makuta's attack on the Great Spirit Mata Nui resulted in that being succumbing to endless sleep. At the same time, Makuta struck at Metru Nui, imprisoning the Matoran population and unleashing a massive earthquake that shook the entire universe. It was only through the valiant efforts of six novice heroes, the Toa Metru — and the sacrifice of the noble hero Toa Lhikan — that the Makuta of Metru Nui was temporarily stopped.

But the damage had already been done. The Great Spirit was asleep, the city of Metru Nui wrecked and abandoned, and the most potent force in existence — the Brotherhood of Makuta — had revealed itself to be an enemy of the light. This was a disaster from which the known universe has still not recovered.

Since that time, Brotherhood members have warred with Toa and the Dark Hunters (for different reasons). The organization continues to gain in strength as they prepare for conquest.

THE INHABITANTS

There were, at one time, one hundred members of the Brotherhood of Makuta. It is believed that number is significantly smaller now, as the Makuta of Metru Nui has weeded out those he felt were insufficiently loyal to his grand design.

It should be emphasized here that "Makuta" is more than just a title — it is also a species name. All the Brotherhood members are part of a species so

ancient that they have evolved beyond the point of having a physical body. The Makuta consist of pure energy, which must be housed in an armored frame. If that armor should be shattered, the energy will leak out and eventually lose cohesion, and the Makuta in question will die.

All Makuta have certain abilities:

Ability to produce kraata: The kraata, sluglike creatures, have the power to infect Kanohi masks and other objects. When exposed to energized protodermis, they transform into Rahkshi armor. Another kraata then serves as "pilot" for the armor.

| **Shape-shifting:** | Makuta can appear in virtually any guise they wish. |
| **Multipowers:** | Makuta have access to the forty-two known Rahkshi powers, including the casting of illusions, teleportation, heat visions, magnetism, weather control, and more. |

Makuta are, as a rule, highly intelligent and skilled inventors and biomechanical engineers. Although they have become associated with darkness, only the Makuta of Metru Nui actually wears a Kanohi Mask of Shadows. Other members wear other masks, all of them with powers best suited to combat.

Different Makuta are charged with conquest of different sections of the universe, all of them answering in the past to the Makuta of Metru Nui (only because he gave birth to the conspiracy in which they all share). Each Makuta has a different style and approach to conflict, meaning that defeating one does not guarantee success against any of the others. Although they are all of the same species, they should not in any way be considered to be copies of each other. Each is cunning and dangerous in his or her own right.

CREATURES OF DESTRAL

VISORAK

The primary Rahi found on Destral, Visorak are spiderlike creatures known for their cunning, high level of organization, and ruthless efficiency. They have been the backbone of the Brotherhood's legions for millennia, as destructive as a barbarian horde and as overwhelming in their power as a biostorm.

Like other Rahi spiders, Visorak can create webs and have powerful pincers. Their most devastating weapon is their venom, which can mutate a victim into a more bestial form of itself. This venom was used against the Toa Metru in Metru Nui, changing them for a time into half-Toa, half-beast Toa Hordika.

The Visorak serve the Brotherhood for one simple reason: The Brotherhood gives them the opportunity to hunt and destroy, which is all a Visorak lives for. It is doubtful the threat of the Visorak will ever end until the last of the species is wiped out.

UPDATE

Initial reports had indicated that the Makuta of Metru Nui was killed following a battle with Takanuva, Toa of Light. But more recent word from Voya Nui would seem to suggest that, though his armor was shattered, the energy that makes up Makuta has yet to dissipate. It was used as a weapon by the Piraka against the Matoran of Voya Nui until their defeat. The vat housing the energy was destroyed, meaning Makuta is now once more in jeopardy of final death. We believe his goal is to somehow use the Mask of Life to attain ultimate power, and that his first step toward this goal may be an effort to obtain a new body to house his energy form.

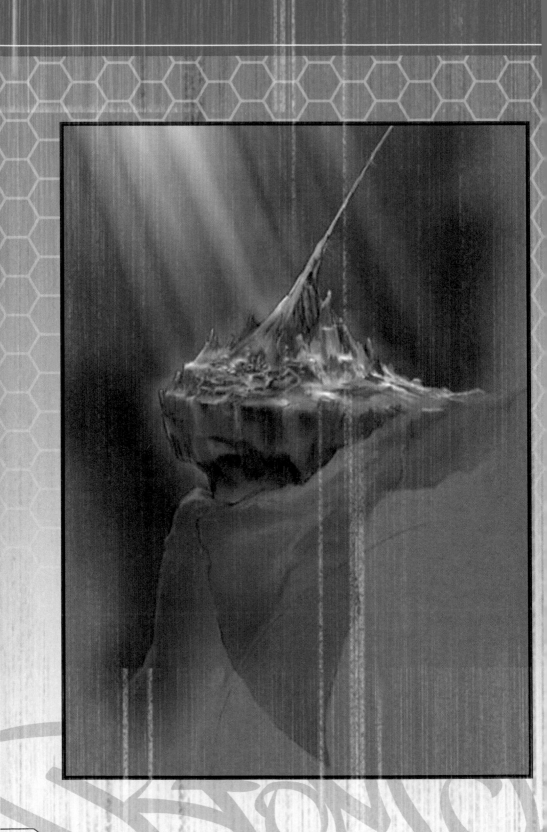

MAHRI NUI

Far beneath the ocean waves is another world, one never before seen by Toa. It is a dark domain, infested by some of the most evil beings in the universe. At one time, it was believed it would serve as their prison for time unending, a place where they would live out eternity and be forgotten. But events beyond our grasp changed all that, and now Mahri Nui and the Pit that surrounds it have become a key battleground in the struggle to save the life of the Great Spirit.

GETTING THERE

The sunken village of Mahri Nui lies beneath a saltwater ocean, the same ocean that surrounds the islands of Voya Nui and Mata Nui. In the depths, however, the waters are quite different, having both corrosive and mutagenic properties that affect both the living and nonliving. As a result, it is an extremely difficult place to survive, let alone thrive. Some beings, like our own Botar, have a natural immunity to the environment of the Pit, but others who wish to journey here must take precautions against prolonged exposure to the waters.

There are two primary means of reaching Mahri Nui itself:

- **Down through the cord:** A tangled, twisted cord of solid protodermis links Mahri Nui below to Voya Nui above. Inside the cord is a complicated and partially flooded tunnel network, home to both land and sea Rahi. The cord comes to an end atop a mountain peak near the village, although there are small openings toward the base through which a traveler can exit. Going this way enables the traveler to adjust gradually to the higher pressures below, but how many dangers may lie along the route remains largely unknown.

- **Up through the Pit:** The waters below Mahri Nui go by many names — the "deep deep," the "black water"— but in truth, they are simply another part of the Pit. At one time, the Pit was an enclosed area well to the south of any known island, a prison for those the Order of Mata Nui deemed beyond redemption. The Great Cataclysm shattered that enclosure, releasing the inhabitants into the waters outside of it. Now they dwell in the murky, dark waters beneath Mahri Nui, longing for revenge on a universe that shuns them. While it is possible to reach Mahri Nui by traveling through the ruins of the prison and up through the black water, it is not recommended.

Nonaquatic beings traveling to Mahri Nui are advised to wear a Great Mask of Water Breathing. If this is impossible, their first stop should be the Fields of Air (see below).

THE LAND

The village of Mahri Nui rests on the base of an inverted triangle of rock, which is wedged in between a pair of curved pillars of stone. Were it ever to become dislodged, it would tumble end over end into the black water, taking all of the Matoran with it.

Note: As best as we can determine, when Mahri Nui sank beneath the sea, its landmass collided with another already there. The result was a fusion of the two, which explains why some of the natural terrain is already well suited to an underwater world.

Mahri Nui's landmass has a number of interesting and important features, including:

- **The Fields of Air:** Located on the outskirts of Mahri Nui, this area teems with plants dubbed "airweed" by the Matoran. Each plant produces bubbles of air that can be merged together to form larger bubbles. The Matoran use Rahi called hydruka (see "Creatures of Mahri Nui") to harvest the air. This is used to create large bubbles around the buildings of Mahri Nui as well as smaller, personal air bubbles for Matoran who venture outside the city.

- **The Pillars of Salt:** Mountains that formed over the centuries from salt deposits in the water. This area is a preferred hunting ground of Takea sharks and so has not been extensively explored by the Matoran.

- **Octo Cave:** A frequent stopping place of the Barraki named Kalmah, this cavern is the source of the sea squid that have plagued the Matoran for so long (see "Creatures of Mahri Nui").

Mahri Nui itself is a medium-size Matoran village, unique in appearance primarily because of the presence of air bubbles over its buildings. Among the most important locations in the village are the Throne of Vision, where Matoran relate any memories they have of their life before the sinking; the Sanctuary, where artifacts that drift down from above are kept; the Fortress, where experiments are done on airweed and air bubbles; and the memorial to those who have fallen victim to sea predators.

HISTORY

The history of Mahri Nui and the Pit is a complex one, but it is vital that a traveler to the area understand it. Following the Great Cataclysm, which shattered the original Pit, Mahri Nui broke off of the island of Voya Nui and sank. It landed on a preexisting piece of rock, crushing a Barraki fortress in the city. The impact was so great that bubbles of air were forced from the airweed, granting the surviving Matoran a small supply of air to help them stay alive.

Shortly after, molten protodermis flowing from Voya Nui cooled in the waters and formed a cord connecting it to Mahri Nui.

The traumatic events leading to their village ending up underwater damaged the memories of the Matoran, leaving them with only fragmentary recollections of their life on the surface. When one of them actually does put the pieces together to form a coherent memory, he is brought to the Throne of Vision to recount the tale, so it can be recorded.

Nevertheless, the displaced Matoran repaired the damage to their homes as best they could and began to build a new life beneath the waves. First priority was maintenance of the Fields of Air, followed by coming up with a defense against sea predators. The two goals were combined when it was discovered that pure air acts like a toxic gas to underwater dwellers. The Matoran created launchers that could fire solid bubbles of air at their enemies.

And enemies they had many of — though the Matoran were not aware of it, their city had landed right in the midst of the Pit. The Barraki initially planned to destroy the village, until they realized that the Matoran had nothing they wanted.

Instead, they contented themselves with picking off Matoran now and then for sport, or unleashing their legions of sea creatures to harass and frighten the villagers.

The Matoran soon learned that there was one hour of the day when no sea predators roamed the waters. This was nicknamed the "safe hour," and became the time when Matoran could tend the Fields of Air or explore outside of the city without fear.

Everything changed dramatically when the Mask of Life drifted down through the water from the shores of Voya Nui. Recovered by the Matoran, it was of immediate interest to the evil Barraki. They saw the mask as an essential first step in reclaiming their lost kingdoms and taking their revenge on the Brotherhood of Makuta (see "Barraki"). They attacked Mahri Nui in force and eventually were able to claim the mask for themselves.

There ends the history of Mahri Nui, for now — and if the mask is not reclaimed from the Barraki soon, it may mark the end of the history of our entire universe.

THE INHABITANTS

At first glance, it is hard to believe that the Matoran of Mahri Nui are related to the Matoran of Voya Nui. Mahri Nui Matoran are taller and stronger, and they bear none of the signs of having been tampered with by Karzahni. Yet they are a part of that group of Matoran first shipped to Karzahni and then shipped out to the mainland, ending up on Voya Nui.

The change in their appearance is actually the only good thing to come out of the disaster they endured. When Mahri Nui sank, the initial exposure to the mutagenic seawater that far below the surface had the effect of undoing many of the changes Karzahni had made. It also destroyed or damaged many of their weapons, although at least some continue to function.

THE BARRAKI

The Pit is also home to the Barraki, easily the greatest threat to both the city and the Mask of Life. At one time, these six beings were warlords and kings, ruling over their own realms on land. Then they attempted to rebel against the Great Spirit Mata Nui and were defeated by the Brotherhood of Makuta. They were banished to the Pit for their crimes.

When the Great Cataclysm set them free of their original place of exile, they were mutated by the ocean waters into the hideous creatures they are today. Now able to breathe only water, they cannot hope to reclaim their kingdoms unless a way is found to reverse their mutation — something they believe the Mask of Life can do. Backed by armies of sea creatures, they have seized the mask and hope to resume their history of conquest in the universe at large.

How any team of Toa can defeat the Barraki remains unclear. Each of them — Pridak, Takadox, Kalmah, Mantax, Ehlek, and Carapar — is a cunning and dangerous foe, with a detailed knowledge of their environment and how

best to make use of it in combat. It will take all of the Toa Inika's skill merely to survive their time in the Pit.

CREATURES OF MAHRI NUI

SEA SQUID

Although the Pit is home to many bizarre creatures, one of the most important to current events below the sea is the sea squid. These small, nasty creatures are bred by the Barraki named Kalmah, in some way we have not yet discovered. Unlike other sea creatures, who simply feed on the bodies of marine life, the sea squid actually feeds on the life force of its prey.

When a sea squid attaches itself to another living thing, the suckers in its tentacles begin to draw out the energy of the unfortunate victim. If the squid is not torn off before it is too late, the prey will die. It is difficult to brand a creature that lives solely by instinct as "evil," but certainly nature has chosen for the sea squid a most painful and brutal way to survive.

Of course, much of the squid's nature can be traced back to their treatment by Kalmah. He makes sure they are kept hungry and hostile. It was also Kalmah

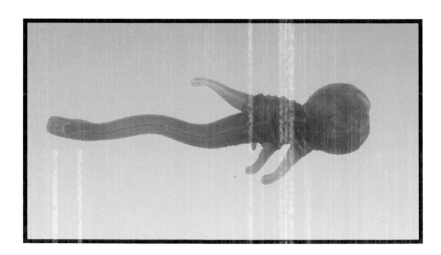

who designed a mechanical launcher that could be used to hurl the squid at potential victims. Such a weapon is now carried by all the Barraki.

As with all the Pit's sea creatures, air is toxic to the squid. While they are small, they are incredibly strong, and it can take great effort to detach one from its chosen prey.

HYDRUKA

Scorpion-like sea creatures, the hydruka are domesticated beasts who serve the Matoran of Mahri Nui by harvesting air bubbles from the airweed. Their mode of defense — launching those bubbles at opponents — inspired the Matoran to build the launchers they use to defend the city.

Hydruka are notoriously sensitive, stubborn, and temperamental. They work at their own pace, and attempts to rush them will either frighten or anger them.

UPDATE

The Mask of Life is now in the claws of the Barraki. This in itself is troubling, but there are signs the mask may be damaged or even on the verge of self-destruction. Upon its capture, it gave off a blinding flash of energy, whose purpose and full effects remain unknown. Contact was lost with our observer in the area, so the Order now has no idea what may be transpiring down below. We fear the worst.